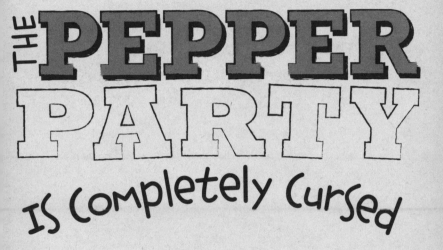

THE PEPPER PARTY

IS Completely Cursed

THE PEPPER PARTY IS JUST GETTING STARTED!

#1 The Pepper Party Picks the Perfect Pet
#2 The Pepper Party Family Feud Face-Off
#3 The Pepper Party Is Completely Cursed

THE PEPPER PARTY

IS Completely Cursed

BY

JAY COOPER

Scholastic Inc.

For my big sis, Teresa, whose
ghost stories scared me silly!

Copyright © 2019 by Jay Cooper

All rights reserved. Published by Scholastic Inc., *Publishers since 1920.* SCHOLASTIC and associated logos are trademarks and/or registered trademarks of Scholastic Inc.

The publisher does not have any control over and does not assume any responsibility for author or third-party websites or their content.

ISBN 978-1-338-29706-5

10 9 8 7 6 5 4 3 2 1   19 20 21 22 23
Printed in U.S.A.   40
First printing, October 2019
Book design by Nina Goffi

CHAPTER 1

Every year, San Pimento went bonkers over Halloween. All across the city, fabric ghosts hung from tree branches, foam gravestones lined the sidewalks, and giant inflatable witches wobbled on every lawn. And everyone always made sure one house was on their

trick-or-treating list . . . the Pepper house!

No one in town had more Halloween spirit. But the Peppers could never agree on *anything*, and their Halloween theme was no exception.

Maria insisted on fairies and glitter, while Annie wanted bloody fangs and evil eyes everywhere. Sal thought a true Pepper Halloween should be themed after his favorite scary movie, *Attack of the Killer Chili*. Since the family couldn't agree, they each decided to do Halloween their own way . . . and the house ended up looking a little mixed-up.

One Pepper in particular took Halloween *very* seriously.

Beta Max planned on making the scariest movies of all time when he grew up. His movies would be bloodier than the bloodiest zombie movies and would make audiences jump higher than Stevie Shpealburger's classic shark movie, *Teeths!* So it's no surprise that Beta thought that Halloween was the coolest of holidays. And every year he made a brand-new, super scary movie to show to the family after they finished trick-or-treating.

This year he had outdone himself.

Beta Max had written a stellar screenplay entitled *Vampire Lizard Mummymen from Mars.* There were thrills, chills, and

1. Sal (father) creating a chili monster on the lawn
2. Maria (9) glitter fairy land
3. Beta (also 9) mummy's tomb
4. Ricky (12) vampire bat band
5. Megs (10) zombie football game
6. Annie (8) giant clown-spider
7. Tee (mom) witch's cauldron
8. Meemaw (ancient) putting up Presto Pepper's old posters
9. Scoochy (2) exploding unicorns

even a romance. Beta thought love stories were kind of gross. But he wanted there to be something for everyone. Mostly the movie was just plain scary! And he was nearly ready to start filming.

He had a big family and truckloads of friends he could use as actors. In fact, he had already cast his big sister Megs in the leading role, as the heroic space marine with fists of gold and a heart of steel. (Or was it the other way around? Yes! She had fists of *steel* and a heart of *gold*!)

What Beta really needed to bring his vision to life were amazing sets and props. *Vampire Lizard Mummymen from Mars* wasn't any old cheesy movie he could make with stuff he found around the house. This one was extra special, and it needed to look that way!

Sadly, Beta was totally broke. He didn't have so much as a dollar to buy supplies to build his film set.

He had hired Annie as his assistant director, since she'd done such a great job on his last movie. Together they would have to find cheap, creative ways to make their scenes spring to life on the screen.

One afternoon, they were lounging in Annie's Halloween clown–spiderweb decoration on the front lawn (she had made it by combining the two scariest things she could think of).

They brainstormed ways they could make their movie.

"We could set up a lemonade stand to raise money," suggested Annie.

"In October? No one buys lemonade in October," Beta glumly replied.

Beta stared at the giant clown-spider's silly red nose, wondering if he could give his vampire lizard mummymen glowing red eyes using some borrowed night-lights from his brother's and sisters' rooms, when Meemaw Pepper hobbled past, barely visible beneath a load of rolled-up posters.

Their grandmother decorated for Halloween by tacking up old posters that belonged to her father, Presto Pepper, on the garage door. Presto had been a famously terrible magician—he had been so bad at magic that people had traveled across the country to watch him screw up his tricks. He'd even been the toast of a European tour, and had famously failed to make Big Ben disappear. (He'd only made the first two floors of the clock tower vanish, and they'd renamed it Not Quite as Big Ben.) When he'd offered to make the crown jewels disappear, the queen politely said no. She was worried she'd never get them back!

But Meemaw loved her father dearly, and since Halloween had been his favorite holiday, she liked to honor him. Beta watched as she slowly unrolled a poster and started putting it up. The poster read, "The Amazingly Terrible Presto Pepper: You Will Believe Your Eyes!"

"Hey, Meemaw," called Beta. "Those old posters are so cool! Why don't we get one framed for the house?"

Meemaw took a step back and smiled at the image of her father losing his grip on a deck of cards. "Pappy liked to make an entrance (usually by tripping over the curtain and falling into the audience). He wouldn't want to be just hangin' around all the time. You'd never give him a second look!" She shook her head. "Nope. After Halloween, I'll put 'em back in the attic along with Presto's other props."

Beta froze, and Annie, who'd been playing with her giant clown-spider's red nose, stopped mid-honk.

"Props?" asked Beta, trying to sound casual.

"Oh, sure," said Meemaw as she tacked another poster to the garage door. "All his doodads and whatchamacallits and magic show sets are up in the attic. My little Sallie's always threatening to throw them out, but then I just give 'im THE GLARE. So they're up there, just collecting dust."

Beta and Annie stared at each other. They were thinking the same thing. And it wasn't that Meemaw's glare could wilt a flower, although it could.

Annie asked in a sweet voice, "Meemaw, would you mind if we used them in a movie we're making?"

Their grandmother smiled. "I think Presto would think that's a mighty fine idea. Just don't break anything . . ." she warned sternly. "Or Presto may come back to haunt you!"

Beta and Annie looked scared.

"HA!" Meemaw hooted. "I'm just pullin' yer legs! HA HA!!!"

With that she pulled out another poster. This one read, "Presto the Not Nearly Amazing! Can He Escape the Water Tank of Doom?" Meemaw shook her head. Apparently, Presto couldn't.

CHAPTER 2

Beta and Annie crept up the steps to the attic. Beta's jaw dropped. How had he not spent more time up here before? This place was super spooky, full of cobwebs, and musty. It was THE BEST.

One of their mother's old dolls sat on a rocking chair and seemed to follow them with

her glass eyes. Annie
shuddered. Creepy dolls
gave her the willies!

Together, they made
their way into the deep-
est part of the attic.

All the way in the back, the pair found what
they were looking for. There were all sorts of
strange, magic-themed backdrops and furniture: boxes for sawing people in half, cabinets
of curiosity, a giant water tank, and a few large
steamer trunks.

Beta began to open the trunks and cried out
with delight.

"Wow! Look at all this stuff! Electricity balls,
trick decks of cards, swords for swallowing . . .
This stuff is great. This is going to be the best
movie EVER!"

Annie tried not to look too closely at the creepy, dark stains on the sawing-people-in-half box—she really, really hoped it was prune juice—and turned her attention to the disappearing cabinet. She opened the door and found a bunch of instructional books on magic. She read titles like *To Appear or To Disappear: That is the Question!* and *Be Back in a Blink!* They were library books that had been checked out in the 1930s and never brought back.

"I guess Presto was better at disappearing than returning," Annie muttered.

In another old trunk, Beta found costumes from Presto's act. Beta pulled out boas, turbans, and a patterned sequin robe. He threw on Presto's red satin-lined cape and top hat. Then he posed in front of a dusty old mirror.

"Behold! I am Presto, the Not Nearly Amazing!"

"Behold! You are Beta Max Pepper, the Super Goofy!" Annie laughed. She glanced at a framed photo of Presto in the same pose. "You know, you do kinda look like him!"

"Oh yeah? Well, we are both entertainers. Maybe I take after our great-grandfather." He added quickly, "Of course, I'm much more talented . . ."

Then something caught Beta's eye: a sheet covering something mysterious that had a roundish shape poking up in the middle. "Hey, what's this?"

Together they lifted the sheet. Beneath it was an ornately carved table with an old crystal ball sitting in the center. Two chairs were set on either side of the table.

Together, Annie and Beta said, "WHOA."

They sat down in the chairs. "Look, there are words on the table!" said Annie.

She read them out loud in a heavy, hypnotic accent. "With this ball you can scry, but do not disturb

the spirits in the crystal, or all your fortunes will become MIS-fortunes!"

She looked up at Beta. "What's *scry* mean?"

"It means using a crystal ball to see the future."

Annie waggled her eyebrows. "Well, if you could see your future, you'd be scrying, too!"

She squinted into the ball.

"I predict . . . Megs will give up sports and become a couch potato!" She looked deeper into the ball. "Maria will be NICE for a change! And Dad's mustache WILL FALL OFF!"

Beta laughed. "Yeah, when pigs fly!"

"Yes! Oink is going to fly!"

They both giggled. The idea of their tubby pet pig flying was ridiculous.

"If you're going to predict crazy stuff, Annie, you shouldn't be so boring about it! It's Halloween—we should really go for it!"

"Be my guest." Annie smiled.

Beta cracked his knuckles and waved his hands over the ball. "I call upon the spirits of the netherworld! Hear me!"

Annie responded in a telephone computer voice. "Bee boo doo! If you'd like to make a call, please hang up and try again."

"Shh! Spirits, I call upon you to let me see the dark futures of the Peppers!"

He looked into the ball, and then his eyes widened. "Ah! I see that Mom will become a scary witch!"

"And Dad will transform into a mindless zombie!"

"Scoochy will turn into a WERE-CHIHUAHUA!"

Annie laughed at this, imagining the baby of the family as a tiny vicious dog-beast.

"Finally, Ricky will find true love . . . IN THE AFTERLIFE!"

Annie clapped. "Bravo!"

Beta stood and took a dramatic, sweeping bow. But as he did, his cape swung around and knocked into the crystal ball.

It happened in slow motion, just like in a movie. The cape whacked the ball, which slowly rolled off its pedestal and across the table. Beta and Annie both reached for it at the same time.

"NOOOOOOOOOO!"

For just a moment the crystal ball wobbled on the edge of the table. Annie and Beta dove for it, knocking into each other and tipping the ball over . . .

. . . and onto the floor, where it shattered into about a million pieces.

Annie and Beta looked at all the smashed fragments of crystal ball in silent horror.

Annie whispered, "Oh no! Beta, we broke Presto Pepper's crystal ball! What are we going to do?"

Beta thought quickly and said, "We pretend it never happened. We take what we need for the movie, sweep the broken glass under the vanity, and we never, ever, *ever* speak of this again."

Annie nodded. "Agreed!"

But as they cleaned up, Beta couldn't help glancing at the warning on the table. He was pretty sure that breaking a crystal ball was just about the most disturbing thing you could do to the spirits inside it.

Good thing fortunes weren't real. They were just pretend . . . like his scary movies.

CHAPTER 3

The next morning was predictably Peppery, meaning totally crazy.

Scoochy played hide-and-seek with Azzie the Chihuahua's favorite chew toy. Mostly she just hid it and teased the small dog. "AZZIE WANT TOY? NO TOY! NO TOY!" Azzie

growled and barked until Scoochy finally gave it back.

Beta's twin sister, Maria, sat at the kitchen table choosing between some glossy headshots she'd had her friend Roger take of her. As her school's mascot, she'd come to crave the spotlight, and now she thought she might branch out into acting. "Do you think I should go with 'beautiful, but I don't care' or 'confident, but whatever'?"

Meemaw, as usual, had lost her dentures, and was currently rummaging around in the fridge looking for them.

Ricky, the oldest Pepper brother, scribbled a tune on some sheets of lined music paper between spoonfuls of cereal. Elvis the lovebird sat on Ricky's shoulder and nodded his approval. Ricky was working on an exciting new project but wouldn't say what it was.

Megs said it had something to do with a new crush.

The Pepper parents, Tee and Sal, had been working on their own secret project for the past month, and were being very hush-hush about the whole thing. Normally Sal would be cooking up a delicious breakfast chili, but he hadn't so much as looked at the stove that morning. Whenever anyone asked where the bacon, eggs, and toast were, he pushed the cereal box toward them without looking away from what Tee was busily scribbling into a leather book.

As Annie reached over for the cereal box, she caught a glimpse of what her mother was writing. It looked like a recipe, except it mentioned how many gallons of brew a black cauldron might hold, and the list of ingredients was all strange herbs. Tee caught Annie snooping. Her mother gave her a creepy smile, and then she snapped the book shut.

Beta padded into the kitchen in his pajamas looking totally wiped out. He'd had terrible nightmares about being chased around the house by the spirits of the crystal ball.

As he slumped into his seat, Meemaw asked him if he'd had any luck finding Presto's old things in the attic as she shook milk off the dentures she'd just found, at the bottom of the carton.

Beta tried to hide his panic over the broken ball. He faked a giant grin. "Yep. Found them.

Very useful. Nothing broken. Everything is not even a little bit broken in the attic!"

Annie nudged him hard and whispered into his ear, "Beta, shhhhh!"

Beta was about to respond, when suddenly they heard a series of thumps from the stairs in the hallway.

THUMP.

BUMP.

BUMPITY BUMP BUMP BUMP!

"YOWCH!!!!!!"

Everyone leapt from the table and ran toward the sound.

It was their older sister Megs. She lay sprawled at the bottom of the stairs, holding her leg and crying.

Tee ran to her. "Megs! Are you all right?"

"I fell down the stairs! My leg really hurts, Mom!"

Tee touched Megs's leg gingerly.

"OWOWOWOWOW!!!" Megs screamed.

"Oh dear, I think it's broken. Pick her up, Sal. Gently! We have to take her to the emergency room." She sighed. "Everyone else, get yourselves ready for school."

Megs continued to cry as her father lifted her up as delicately as he could. "But I have the froosbetball championship next week! I can't miss it! I'm team captain!"

Tee shook her head sadly. "You probably won't be playing sports for a while, sweetie."

This made Megs burst into a fresh batch of tears.

Tee and Sal carried Megs as gently as they could to the family car, which was actually a food truck called the Chili Chikka-Wow-Wow.

As they drove off to the hospital, Sal turned on the food truck's loudspeaker and did an impression of an ambulance siren to cheer Megs up. *"Wooooooo WooooOOOOoooo!"*

When the rest of the kids were dressed, they walked together to school in glum silence (well, all except Scoochy, who didn't like school or clothing). None of them had ever seen Megs cry before.

Beta and Annie walked a ways behind Ricky and Maria.

"That's some tough luck," said Beta. "Megs not being able to play sports is almost as bad as Dad not being able to make his chili!"

Suddenly, a realization dawned on him. "Agh! Megs was the hero of my movie! Now I have to find someone else to play the space marine with fists of gold and a heart of steel. Sorry, got that backward again. Why do I keep doing that?!"

Annie stopped cold.

Beta asked, "What's wrong?"

"The very *first* thing I predicted yesterday on Presto's crystal ball was that Megs would spend less time playing sports . . . and now she's BROKEN HER LEG."

Beta scoffed. "Oh, come on, Annie, don't be so superstitious. That's just a silly coincidence."

"I don't know, Beta. The curse said if we disturbed the spirits, our fortunes would become MIS-fortunes, and Megs breaking her leg sure seems like a misfortune to me!"

"Hocus-pocus. Mumbo jumbo. Crisscross applesauce! Don't give it another thought," said Beta with a smile. But inside, he was worried. Could the fortunes be . . . coming true? No way!

He stewed about it all day, and by the time he got home, he still wasn't feeling entirely confident, but he decided to keep putting on a brave face.

Especially when he saw Megs with her new cast and crutches. She was propped up on the couch eating a bowl of ice cream.

Annie gasped at the sight and nudged Beta. "Look! It's just like my prediction!" she whispered in his ear. "Megs has become a couch potato!"

"Wow," said Maria, putting down her book bag. "Your leg is actually broken? Like, the bone is totally snapped?"

Megs frowned. "Yeah, and the doctor says there's no way it'll be healed in time for the froosbetball finals. The team captain will have to sit this one out, I guess."

Megs wasn't just team captain for the San Pimento froosbetball team, she had invented the sport. It was a combination of basketball and Frisbee, where players dribbled and flung a flattened basketball through a hoop. The strange sport had become really popular in San Pimento.

Annie gave Beta a guilty glance, but he waved her off.

"What actually happened?" Beta asked.

"It was the weirdest thing. I was getting ready to come down for breakfast, reading your movie script, Beta, and then I stepped on this."

She held up a shard of curved broken glass.

Beta gasped. It was a piece of the crystal ball.

"I didn't have any shoes on, and I was hopping in pain—right at the top of the stairs. Next thing you know . . . boom boom crash!"

She looked at the glass. "Any ideas where it came from?"

Beta and Annie shook their heads *really* hard.

"Anyway, Beta, you'll have to find someone else to fight the vampire lizard mummy dudes for you. Sorry."

Beta furrowed his brow.

But Maria just smiled.

CHAPTER 4

That week, Beta started building his movie set for *Vampire Lizard Mummymen from Mars*. He and Annie transformed the garage into the Mars space station, using a lot of Presto's props and furniture. They had combined this with some of Sal's old cooking equipment and spare

ventilation tubing to create a space station that looked old-fashioned and futuristic at the same time.

However, they now had a huge setback. Beta and Annie had to recast their lead. Annie had pinned an audition sign-up sheet on the school bulletin board. Beta hoped they'd have a bunch of good candidates for the part.

In the meantime, Maria had offered to help him work on the set. Maria was normally pretty bossy, especially with Beta, but today she was all smiles.

She asked sweetly, "Would you like me to connect the tubing to the water tank? Or do you want me to start painting the creepy Mars landscape on the tarp?"

"Hmm. Good question . . . Maybe the creepy Mars backdrop? I'm thinking weird red mist, and strange rock formations that could maybe be old statues worn down over a hundred thousand years!"

"Your wish is my command. I am just a humble assistant." Maria bounced away to get the paint supplies ready.

"Wow," said Beta. "Thanks!"

Annie walked into the garage, surprised to see her sister there.

"Hi, Maria, what are you doing here?"

"Helping Beta! I'm going to paint the backdrop."

"But . . . whenever I ask you to help me paint something, you give me that look that makes me go hide."

Maria had inherited THE GLARE from Meemaw.

"Well, from now on I'll be sure to give you

this look, instead." Maria flashed her biggest, brightest smile. Somehow, it was scarier than THE GLARE. As if by magic, Maria made a plate of baked goods appear. "Chocolate chip cookie? I made them fresh!"

Beta ran over, grabbed three, and stuffed them into his mouth. "Fanks, Mawia, fese are freat!" He spat crumbs all over Maria's face.

Maria wiped them off and forced a smile. "My . . . pleasure, Beta." Annie couldn't believe that Maria didn't kill him.

With a sudden, sinking feeling, she was pretty sure she knew why.

"Um, Maria, the director and the assistant director need a moment to confer about the, um, tone of the movie. We're having some . . . artistic differences."

Maria, who would normally never go along with being left out of a conversation, smiled and snapped her fingers. "Tell you what, you two have your private conference, and I'll go make us a batch of fresh-squeezed lemonade to go with the chocolate chip cookies. How does that sound?"

Beta smiled. "Great, sis! What has gotten into you lately?"

Maria shrugged. "I guess I've just cleaned up my *act*, shall we say?"

Beta and Annie watched her go.

Beta nodded approvingly. "I really like this new, improved Maria."

Annie grabbed his shoulders and shook him hard. "Beta! Don't you realize? Maria is acting *nice*. She's acting *friendly*. She's not being *bossy*!"

Beta said, "I know! Isn't it great?"

"No! It's not great! It's all part of THE CURSE!"

Beta raised an eyebrow. "Curse?"

"Yes! Isn't it obvious? We've been *cursed*. And I think it's all because we broke Presto's crystal ball!"

"You're kidding, right?"

"Nope." On her fingers, she counted off the facts. "First I predicted that Meg would stop playing sports, and then she broke her leg. Second, I predicted that Maria would be *nice* . . . and she's making us fresh-squeezed lemonade . . . *in late October*!"

Beta stopped and thought about it. "It was my turn to do dishes last night, and she volunteered to do them for me. Maria never offers to do my dishes! Even that one time when I had the chicken pox, she *still* made me do them. I practically had to wear a hazmat suit."

"I think we've been cursed by the spirit of Presto Pepper for breaking his crystal ball!"

Beta's jaw dropped. "What was the next prediction we made?"

"That Dad would lose his mustache."

"Well, that'll never happen!" Beta laughed. Then he laughed some more. In fact, he laughed so hard, he was worried he might have an accident. "All this talk about lemonade has made me need to use the restroom. I'll be right back."

As he ran up the stairs, he began to compose the score for *Vampire Lizard Mummymen from Mars* in his head. He hummed it as he headed to the bathroom: "Bum budda dum dum dum budda dum dummmm . . ."

"Hiya, son."

"Hey, Dad." Beta gave his father a high five, then kept walking and humming.

Suddenly, he jerked to a stop. "Dad, could you turn around, please?" he croaked. His throat had gone dry.

Sal stopped and very, very slowly turned around.

Beta couldn't believe what he was seeing . . . or rather, he couldn't believe what he was NOT seeing!

His father's beard and handlebar mustache were GONE.

"YAAAAAAAHHHHHH!" screamed Beta.

"AAAAAAAHHHHHH!" Sal screamed back. He looked around frantically, as though a bat was loose in the hallway.

"Where's . . . where's your . . ." Beta's hand shook as he pointed at the lack of facial hair on his dad's face.

Sal asked, "What? What? Is something in my beard?"

Sal felt his face. He even tried twirling his mustache, BUT THERE WAS NOTHING LEFT TO TWIRL!

"My mustache! It was there last night, but now it's gone!"

Beta screamed again, ran into the bathroom, and slammed the door shut behind him.

Tee poked her head out of their room. "That was just plain mean."

Sal chuckled. "It *was* mean. It was also fun."

Tee smiled. "You look good! That banker will be very impressed!"

"You know the old Pepper rule: Dress to impress, but don't overdress, because it'll impress less!"

Sal twirled the shaving razor he had hidden

 behind his back and whistled the tune that Beta had been humming.

CHAPTER 5

That night, after everyone went to bed, Beta and Annie met secretly in Beta's room.

"Okay. We are officially cursed!!!" Beta told his sister. "So what do we do now?"

"I have no idea," Annie said. "No one will ever believe us. Plus, if we tell anyone about the curse, we'd have to admit we broke Presto's crystal ball."

Beta tried to be sensible. "All the misfortunes we've seen so far have been kind of normal. Missing the froosbetball championship, a nice Maria, and a mustache-less Dad is way different from zombies, witches, and werewolves . . ."

"Were-*Chihuahua*," Annie corrected.

"Totally. Now that I think about it, none of those other things could possibly happen anyway. I bet we're in the clear from here on out."

"You're right, Beta."

There was a scratching at the door. Beta opened it cautiously, a little worried about what might be waiting on the other side. But it was just the Pepper pets. They all looked hungry, but their pet pig, Oink, looked particularly put out.

Annie grimaced. "Geez Louise! I was so focused on this curse stuff that I totally forgot it was my turn to feed the pets! And you know how Oink gets when he misses a meal . . ."

Oink's round belly answered with a loud, testy rumble.

Annie ran off to feed them.

"Hey! Don't leave me all by myself!" Beta ran after her. All this talk of curses had totally creeped him out.

The two crept downstairs with the animals close on their heels.

At the foot of the steps, Annie and Beta stopped.

Someone was moving about, even though it was long after everyone had gone to bed.

In the dim light, they recognized their mother. Tee came from the kitchen with a number of glass vials from her spice rack, and some fresh plant cuttings from her garden in the backyard.

"These herbs will be perfect for my witch's brew!" She let out a high-pitched shrieking sound. It sounded a lot like a witch's cackle.

She wiped her nose with a tissue before stuffing the ingredients into a bag and slipping out the door.

Annie and Beta gave each other a quick look, and then ran to the living room and peeked out the window. They just caught a glimpse of their mother disappearing into the darkness in a long black cloak.

"Do we really have to follow her?" groaned Beta.

"Do we really have a choice?" Annie frowned right back.

"I guess not." Beta sighed.

In the dim glow of the streetlights, Beta and Annie trailed their mother down the sidewalk at a safe distance. They didn't want her to see them.

After several blocks, Tee stopped in front of a dark, looming building that all the kids in town knew and feared: the Black Cat Hotel!

The Black Cat Hotel was a legend in San Pimento. The builders had wanted to create a hotel that would attract people with its creepy and spooky design, but they had done too good a job—no one had been brave enough to sleep there overnight! So the hotel had gone bankrupt and closed. The glass windows had been painted black, and the stone panthers that

decorated the entrance always seemed to be growling at passersby. The hotel had sat empty in the middle of San Pimento for nearly one hundred years.

Now Beta and Annie were shocked to see their mother walk straight up the steps as if she owned the place! She pulled an ornate iron key from her bag that she used to unlock the door, and made that strange cackling sound again! She pulled a pointed black hat out of her bag and a shawl decorated with moons and stars, which she wrapped tightly around herself. Then she slipped through the door.

"Our mother is a witch," whispered Annie.

"Don't say that," Beta replied. "Even if it's true."

They crept up the hotel steps, and Beta used his fingernail to scratch off a bit of old

paint from the windows so they could peek inside. They could just make out their mother standing over a large cauldron in the center of the hotel lobby. She cackled as she lit a fire beneath it. With a dramatic flourish, she threw the herbs she had brought from the house into the cauldron. Her face was creepy in the firelight.

"Yep." Beta nodded. "Our mother's a witch, all right."

The pair ran back to the house as fast as they could. They were both pretty freaked out by what they had seen at the hotel.

As they hustled up the front steps to the house, something suddenly jumped out of the shadows at Annie. She reacted instinctively.

"GET OFF ME, YOU ICKY WITCH!" she screamed, and threw the thing off of her with all her might.

Oink wasn't expecting that.

The very hungry pig had watched Beta and Annie sneak off after their mother. But Oink

was patient. He'd sat on the front stoop and waited for them to come back and feed him his dinner, his stomach growling loudly all the while. When he finally saw the pair running up the sidewalk, he got so excited that he leapt out to hug them. He was surprised, to say the least, when Annie tossed him like a tubby basketball!

He spun head over tail into the clown-spider's web, bounced right off it, and sailed high over Beta's and Annie's heads.

"OOOOOIIIIIINNNNKKKK!" he cried as he flew, creating a silhouette against the moon.

The two watched him together.

Beta sighed. "Oink will fly."

Annie sighed. "The curse is real . . . and it's not over yet."

CHAPTER 6

There was only one thing to do: research at the library.

Annie and Beta asked the librarian where they might find the section on curses.

The librarian raised an eyebrow. She sent them to the New Age section, which was where they shelved books about magic, fortune-telling, and jinxes.

Annie scanned one side of the aisle, and Beta took the other side.

"Here's a book about how to avoid spell-casters, called *Witches Get Stitches*."

Beta shook his head. "No way! We don't want to hurt Mom!"

"How about *Poltergeists, And Other Super Weird Words*?"

"Pull that. Wait a minute . . . here we go!" Beta held a book out to Annie called *Being Cursed Is Just the Worst: A Practical Guide to Becoming Uncursed*.

"That's the ticket!" she agreed.

They were just about to check out the book when

they heard a familiar voice. They peeked around the corner.

It was their big brother, Ricky, sitting at a table with a girl they didn't recognize. She wore all black, a bunch of eye shadow, and black lipstick, and had jet-black hair.

"I dunno, do you really think I'm ready, Evelyn?" Ricky asked.

"I think you're *more* than ready," the girl replied.

"I'm kind of nervous. I've never done anything like this before." Ricky looked down at the table.

"Everyone's nervous at first. But then they embrace it! Trust me, you're going to love it in The Afterlife!"

Beta moaned. "Oh brother. Annie, we have to stop this curse!"

CHAPTER 7

Beta and Annie spent the day reading up on "uncursing."

Apparently, breaking curses was compli-cated. Each curse needed to be broken in its own way. Which sort of uncursing method should they try?

There was the fire method, which involved lighting cursed objects aflame. But they weren't allowed to play with matches.

There was the burial method, where they'd have to bury their family members alive. Way too dirty!

Annie found just one method that looked promising. The Curse-Dance-Off method had been created by a pilgrim family to free their mother from a rare case of poultry cursing. After baking a hexed chicken, their mother had begun to cluck uncontrollably. Her head began to spin, and she had even begun to lay her own eggs! She tried to flap her wings and fly, but luckily that didn't even work for regular chickens.

The pilgrim kids had decided to break the curse by dancing it away. To their amazement,

it had worked! The steps of the Curse-Dance-Off were written in the book. But the trick of this particular uncursing was you couldn't perform it just *anytime*. You had to do it right when the curse was taking effect. And you had to do it in a circle around the person who was cursed.

"So, we have to do this dance when the next one of our family members changes into something monstrous?"

"I guess so," said Annie.

"Well, when's that?"

Annie shrugged. "Hard to know. But we should practice the dance and get it ready."

Beta read the description and shook his head. "I don't know, Annie. It's a pretty dumb dance."

Annie snapped the book closed angrily. "Do you want to break this curse or not, Beta?"

"Sorry." Beta was just grumpy because this curse was causing major delays in his movie production.

They practiced the Curse-Dance-Off. It really was a ridiculous dance.

~~~~~~~~~~~~~~~

That night at dinner, they had to order Chinese. Normally Sal made chili for dinner, but he'd been strangely absent the past week, and no one had caught a glimpse of him all day, even though his food truck, the Chili Chikka-Wow-Wow, sat unused in the driveway.

Megs asked their mother, "Where's Dad?" as she scooped some noodles onto her plate.

Tee poured Megs a steaming cup of tea. "Oh, he'll be home shortly. Now drink this, dear. I brewed it with special healing herbs for your leg. It's practically magical!" She cackled like a witch again, "Nyah ha ha hachoo!"

Beta and Annie shot each other nervous glances.

Just then a shadow loomed in the doorway. It was their father, looking as though someone had buried him and dug him up again. Dirt was caked in his hair, his clothes were a muddy mess, and he was coated in soot.

Sal grumbled something under his breath. It sounded a lot like, "*Must . . . eat . . . brains . . .*"

Beta nearly dropped his plate on the floor. "What did you say?!!"

Sal looked up. Pieces of dirt fell from his head. "I said, 'dust, heat, drains.' Sorry, I was just talking to myself. I'm gonna go get cleaned up."

Beta whispered to his sister as Sal lurched up the stairs, "You heard him say 'must eat brains,' right?"

Annie nodded. "Another one bites the dust."

Sal returned to the table, *mostly* cleaned up. He looked dead on his feet. His face was weirdly pale, and his eyes were red-rimmed. He slumped into his chair like a sack of potatoes.

"What can I get you for dinner, honey?"

He grunted and pointed to the container of barbecued ribs.

Tee filled a plate with ribs and fried rice, and placed it in front of Sal. But she had to step away quickly when he immediately tore into his dinner like he hadn't eaten in years. He grunted and growled as he ripped the meat off the bones with his teeth. And he didn't even bother with a fork when he shoveled the fried rice into his mouth. He cleaned his plate in minutes and then licked his lips and groaned, "More meat!"

The entire family stared at him in shocked horror!

~~~~~~~~~~~~~~~~~~

After dinner, Beta and Annie had offered to do the dishes so that they could confer.

Annie whispered, "The Peppers are dropping like flies! Dad's totally zombified. We have to be ready when this curse strikes again!"

Beta whispered back, "I just hope we have time to do the uncursing dance when it does!"

Just then, the pair heard growling from the other room, followed by Scoochy's loud laughter.

"Scoochy," they heard their mother say, "give that poor little dog his stuffed toy back. If he gets much angrier he might bite you!"

Annie and Beta looked at each other. There was only one way for Scoochy to become a were-Chihuahua, and that was to be bitten by Azzie!

Azzie's growling became barking.

Suddenly, Scoochy wasn't giggling anymore. She was shrieking!

Beta and Annie dropped the takeout into the trash and ran back to the dining room just

in time to see Scoochy running away from the table with Azzie hot on her trail.

Beta and Annie ran after the Chihuahua, who had taken off after the toddler.

They had to surround the two of them and do the Curse-Dance-Off just as the curse took effect. The problem was catching them in time!

By the time Beta and Annie reached the living room, Scoochy and Azzie were in the hallway. And by the time Beta and Annie made it to the hallway, Scoochy and Azzie had already climbed the stairs.

The siblings took the steps two at a time, and had nearly caught up with their sister and dog when tragedy struck. One minute Annie was running full steam ahead, and the next she was yelling "OW!" and falling to the floor.

Beta tripped over his sister and landed with a thud in front of the open bathroom door . . .

. . . just in time to see Scoochy leap into the bathtub followed by the enraged Chihuahua.

The bathtub was quiet for a moment. Then Beta heard a low growl and a snap followed by

a long wail. Azzie jumped out of the tub with his toy, and padded past Beta with his head held high.

Tee poked her head into the bathroom. Scoochy was crying and holding out her hand, displaying two tiny puncture wounds.

She kissed Scoochy on the head. "Always remember the Pepper rule, Scoochy: A bite in the hand is worth two in the tush!"

Tee already had disinfectant and a bandage at the ready. She picked up Scoochy, soothed her cries, and hugged her.

Beta crawled back to Annie in defeat. "Well, we were too late to stop the curse . . . again! You almost had them. What happened?"

Annie held up another shard of the crystal ball. "The curse happened. I stepped on this."

The two slumped against the hallway wall.

Beta asked, "Think she'll turn into a complete Chihuahua during the full moon, or just a little . . . poochie?"

Scoochy toddled out of the bathroom, eyes still damp with tears. She stopped to scratch behind her ears like a dog, then continued to toddle on her way.

Scratch!
Scratch!

"I just hope the Scoochy Pooch doesn't think she can curl up at the end of my bed," said Annie. "Azzie takes up enough space as it is!"

CHAPTER 8

As Halloween approached, Beta and Annie kept a close eye on Ricky. Their brother was the only one the curse hadn't affected, so he was their one chance to break the curse and save the family!

The two took turns spying on their big brother at school, where he was spending an

awful lot of time with this Evelyn girl. Beta had a sneaking suspicion that Evelyn wasn't all she was cracked up to be. In fact, he was worried that she was secretly a vampire! He should know: He'd done a ton of research on them while preparing for his film *Vampire Lizard Mummymen from Mars*.

First, her skin was very pale. Vampires were always very pale, being undead and all. Second, she wore A LOT of black. Total vampire giveaway. Also, she seemed to avoid the sun like the plague.

But Beta became totally convinced when he spied on Ricky and Evelyn at lunch one day. He'd safely hidden himself behind a cafeteria trash can close enough to them that he could overhear their conversation.

Ricky chowed down on pizza and fries, but Evelyn was making faces at her tuna fish sandwich.

Ricky asked, "Is something wrong with your lunch?"

Evelyn shrugged. "It's fine, I guess. But what I really want is some of that pizza!"

Ricky held the slice toward her. "Take a bite!"

Evelyn smiled. "Aww, thanks! Is there garlic on it?"

"No. Why?"

"I'm seriously allergic to it."

Now, if there's one thing that every vampire expert can agree upon, it's that vampires are always, always, ALWAYS allergic to garlic.

Evelyn was most *definitely* a vampire.

A voice behind Beta made him jump nearly a foot in the air.

It was Maria. Nice, *cursed* Maria, who was frankly becoming a bit of a nuisance. Beta kind of missed the old Maria, who was bossy and had no time for him at school. Sadly, this new one did, and was totally blowing Beta's cover.

"Beta, why are you hiding behind a trash can? Is someone picking on you?"

She called out angrily to the cafeteria, "If you're trying to pick on my brother, you better find someone your own size. Try picking on me and see how *that* turns out for you!"

Beta hissed for her to be quiet.

But it was too late. Everyone in the entire cafeteria stopped mid-mouthful and stared at
them. He stood up awkwardly from behind the
trash can.

Evelyn leaned in to Ricky. "Is that your
brother?"

Ricky nodded. "Yep. And my sister."

"Huh. I'm an only child."

"Lucky," said Ricky flatly.

Evelyn asked, "Can I have a fry?" She dipped
it in ketchup. "Don't you think that ketchup
looks just like blood?" She smiled and took a
bite.

Beta went pale. Evelyn was a vampire and
planned to make Ricky her undead boyfriend!

~~~~~~~~

Back home, things had gone from cursed to
worse!

Scoochy had *definitely* been turned into a were-Chihuahua. She'd stopped trying to get Azzie's toy and had started running around on all fours chasing their cat, Lacey, instead. If that wasn't bad enough, Scoochy had come down with the worst case of fleas the family had ever seen!

CURSED! CURSED! CURSED! WAVE! NICE, BUT CURSED!

Their mom left nightly for the Black Cat Hotel with herbs from her garden in her pointy hat and witch's shawl . . . and her continued screechy cackling had started to fray Beta's and Annie's nerves!

Meanwhile, Sal looked more and more zombified with every passing day! His skin had gone from pale to greenish. He shambled in and out of the house at odd hours of the night, and when he came home, he was always covered in grime. Once or twice his shirt was torn—just like a zombie's would be. But worst of all, he still didn't have any interest in making chili! He definitely wasn't the father they knew and loved anymore.

All the while, Beta still had a movie to make. *And* he still needed a lead actor.

He gave the part to Maria. Since he couldn't seem to get rid of her, he decided he might as well use her!

Maria didn't have muscles like Megs, but when it came to playing a hard-nosed, bossy space marine, she was totally up to the challenge.

When she battled the army of vampire lizard mummymen, Maria was more than ready. She had trained hard to be the San Pimento mascot, and had no problem flipping and

kicking and wrestling just as an actual space marine might. And no one could sell sarcastic lines like Maria! Sarcasm was *practically* a second language for her.

In short, Maria turned out to be a surprisingly great movie action hero.

Of course, the hero the family really needed was one who could save them from Great-Grandfather Presto's curse. And since one wasn't magically appearing out of Presto's top hat, it looked like it was up to Beta and Annie!

CHAPTER 9

Just two days before Halloween, the curse finally came for their brother. Annie, Beta, Maria, and Beta's friends had spent the day filming the movie's final climactic scene in the garage, and most of the actors were covered in scaly lizard makeup and fake blood (in other words, ketchup).

It had been a long day, but a really good one. They had officially wrapped the movie! Beta explained to the group that *wrapped* was movie lingo for finishing.

To celebrate, Beta went to the kitchen to get the bottle of sparkling cider, but when he shut the refrigerator door, he saw something that made him drop the bottle, which landed on his toe.

"Owowowow!" he shouted.

Annie came running.

"Are you okay?" she asked frantically. "Are you cursed? DID DAD EAT YOUR BRAINS???"

Beta could only point at

the refrigerator as he hopped around the kitchen in pain.

A note was taped to the door. It read:

Hey guys,

Tonight at 8 o'clock sharp at the Black Cat Hotel, I'm finally going to join THE AFTERLIFE.

It is going to be a big change for Mom and Dad, so please be on time . . . or you may be sorry forever!

Ricky

Beta looked at the time. It was 7:30 already! That meant they only had a half hour to find Ricky and stop the curse!

He grabbed Annie and searched the house.

But Ricky was already gone. So were Sal, Tee, and Scoochy.

Back in the kitchen, they found Meemaw and Maria pouring glasses of cider for everyone in the cast.

"Pour one for me, too," Beta heard Megs say. "I may not technically be *in* the cast, but I'm wearing one!"

"Forget about the cider," cried Beta. "We have to get down to the Black Cat Hotel and stop that curse!"

"What are you talking about?" asked Megs.

Maria sighed. "Curse?"

Meemaw, who had misplaced her hearing aid, shouted, "WHAT? WHAT WAS THAT?"

"We don't have time to explain," said Beta. "But trust us. If we don't get down there right away, Ricky is going to turn into a vampire!

Dad's already a flesh-eating ZOMBIE, Scoochy's a were-Chihuahua, and Mom's a witch!"

The vampire lizard mummymen were quiet for a moment, and then they all shouted, "AWESOME!!!!"

Beta agreed it would have been awesome if it were a movie. But living in a real-life horror movie was most definitely NOT awesome!

At precisely 7:58, Beta and Annie burst through the doors of the Black Cat Hotel with the rest of their crew following closely behind. Even on crutches, Megs outran most of them.

Inside the hotel, candles flickered, but it was still very dark.

A pair of large, pale hands emerged from the shadows and grabbed Annie's and Beta's shoulders. Then a green face appeared. It was their dad! Sal moaned, "HAIRY OPEN BRAINS!"

Beta and Annie screamed and ran past him into the hotel lobby.

Megs and Maria couldn't quite understand why their father shouting *Happy opening* should cause such a reaction in their brother and sister. But they shrugged and followed them anyway.

The Black Cat Hotel's lobby was huge and as spooky as they'd always imagined it would be. Candles with melting wax cast a dim, creepy light over everything. Bats hung from the chandelier and portraits of ghouls lined the walls. Cobwebs clung to the legs of velvet couches and chairs. It was exactly what you'd expect in a vampire's lair!

Beta and Annie saw a number of shadowy figures just beyond the candlelight. Their mother stood at the witches' cauldron, stirring it with her large wooden spoon. She had

transformed completely into a witch. She cackled loudly and pointed a broom toward the center of the room, where a pair of coffins sat.

Beta and Annie screamed again and hugged each other tightly as the coffin lids began to creak open and a cold mist slowly filled the room.

Evelyn rose out of one coffin, and Ricky rose out of the other. Both were dressed like vampires! Well, Evelyn was dressed the way she *always* dressed, but now Ricky was dressed that way, too! He wore Presto's black cape over an open black shirt and black jeans. He was even wearing eyeliner . . . although you couldn't see it beneath his long hair.

Beta and Annie knew it might be too late to save their poor family, but they had to try. If they didn't do their Curse-Dance-Off RIGHT NOW, they'd be stuck in a family of vampires, ghouls, were-Chihuahuas (and nice Marias) forever!

BE WARNED! If you've never seen a Curse-Dance-Off live, it is possibly the goofiest, silliest dance ever created.

Beta and Annie ran over to either side of Ricky and Evelyn.

Together they counted to three and began.

First the pair stomped like giants and bellowed, "BOOMBEDY DOOMBEDY, THIS

CURSE GO SOON-BEDY!" in their deepest voices. Then they sang, "WOOKA WOOKA WOOKA," and hopped about the room with their eyes practically popping from their heads. Next they hooked arms and do-si-do'd while crossing their eyes and sticking out their tongues.

According to their library book, *Being Cursed Is Just the Worst*, these moves would catch the curse with its guard down.

Next Beta and Annie fell to the marble floor and pretended to run in a circle, chanting, "Whoop whoop whoop," over and over again.

After this, on their hands and knees, they donkey kicked with their back legs in a circle

around Ricky and Evelyn and cried, "Heehaw!" This symbolized kicking the curse to the curb.

Then they got back on their feet and flapped their arms like birds, calling out, "AOOGA AOOGA AOOGA," like an old-fashioned car horn. Some of the book's experts said this would scare the curse away for good. Others said it was just really, really embarrassing.

Next they did the twist. Experts are still unsure how a group of pilgrim children learned a popular dance craze from the 1960s.

They finished by howling at the moon like a pair of wolves.

That is the dance that Beta Max Pepper and Annie Pepper did in the candlelight.

Beta and Annie bent over and tried to catch their breath. Slowly their eyes adjusted to the dim light, and when they looked up, they saw that all the shadowy figures weren't monsters or werewolves or even vampires.

They were just their neighbors and friends, holding tea and cake. No one knew whether they should clap or laugh. Jaws hung open in disbelief. One person coughed.

Ricky stepped out of his coffin and walked up to a microphone that Beta hadn't seen standing there.

"Um, thank you, Beta and Annie, for that

really . . . *interesting* . . . warm-up act," he said. "Welcome, everyone. I'm Ricky and this is Evelyn. And we are The Afterlife. Thanks for coming out tonight to the grand opening of my mom's new shop, Tee's Teas at the Black Cat Café. She and my dad have been working on it for months. So please buy one of my mom's special 'witch's brew teas,' and remember to tip your server. Thank you!"

He sat down next to a set of drums that Beta had been too freaked out to notice.

"Let's hit it!" shouted Evelyn, who Beta also now realized was holding *an electric guitar.*

With that, Ricky and Evelyn launched into their opening number. Evelyn played guitar and crooned into the microphone. Ricky followed her on the drums and sang backup

vocals. Their music was Gothic and haunting, and really rockcd!

Beta was embarrassed beyond belief. He and Annie had gotten everything wrong, and they'd made total fools of themselves. But he didn't care. "You know, this would sound really great as soundtrack music for *Vampire Lizard Mummymen from Mars*."

Annie grabbed two programs and handed one to Beta.

"*The Afterlife* is the name of their *band*, Beta. Evelyn's not a vampire. She's a rock 'n' roll star!"

CHAPTER 10

Tee's Teas at the Black Cat Café was having a stellar opening night celebration. There was a very long line waiting for Tee's specially brewed witch-themed tea, which she ladled into cups from her large cauldron. Opening a creepy-themed café in a spooky old hotel right before Halloween had been a stroke of genius!

The Afterlife played their hearts out. To be fair, a lot of their songs could have been written by vampires. The crowd's favorite was a ballad called "It Sucks to Be Loved by You."

The vampire lizard mummymen stood right up front and danced along.

The rest of the Pepper family sat in a circle on couches so that Beta and Annie could explain themselves.

They told the tale of Presto's curse from beginning to end, starting with the crystal ball and ending with them doing the most embarrassing dance of all time in front of a standing-room-only crowd.

"You actually thought you'd brought a curse on the family?" asked Tee.

Beta and Annie nodded. "We found a book that told us how to break it. The dance once cured a mother who had been cursed into becoming a chicken."

"How, exactly?"

"It made her laugh so hard that she completely forgot about the curse," said Beta.

"Well, it *is* a pretty funny dance," agreed Megs.

All of the Peppers nodded.

"But what I don't understand is how our

predictions seemed to come true," said Beta. "Megs, we predicted you'd give up sports, and then you broke your leg!"

Megs scoffed. "That's not true at all! The minute I knew I was out of the froosbetball tournament, I joined the competitive robotics club and set up a paper football league in the lunchroom! No sports? *Ew!*"

"Okay, okay," said Beta. "But Maria has been really weirdly nice, in a definite un-Maria-like way."

"Yeah, dork, because I wanted to be the lead in your movie! And now that we've wrapped, I can go back to being bossy. Go get me a scone."

All of this made too much sense to Beta to actually make sense.

He pointed at Scoochy. "And the were-Chihuahua?"

At that very moment, Scoochy scratched behind her ear with her leg.

"Oh, that," sighed Tee. "Azzie gave her fleas."

"But Dad's mustache fell off! THAT HAPPENED!"

Sal laughed. "I shaved it so your mom and I could get a loan from the bank to open this

café. It's been her dream for years to open her own tea shop. I wanted to look like a proper businessman. I even put on a suit! Besides, the mustache will grow back in no time!"

Tee hugged Sal tightly. "As for your father looking like a zombie, it's true. But that's because I've had him working late nights renovating the hotel while I got the business together! He's not a brain-eating zombie, he's just really, REALLY tired! I've had him on his hands and knees in the basement of this old place getting the heating and the plumbing to work properly!"

Annie smacked her forehead when she realized that they had misheard their dad. Sal hadn't grunted, "Must eat brains!" He was actually muttering about all the *dust* and the *heat* and the *drains* he had to deal with over at the hotel.

Tee continued, "And thank goodness, too, because I had really caught the worst cold

working all month in this freezing hotel without any heat! NYAH HA HA HACHOO!" Tee blew her nose into a tissue.

Beta realized now that those witchy cackles were actually just Mom's biggest sneezes ever!

"Gesundheit," said Megs cheerfully.

Indeed, Sal was so exhausted from all his hard work that he had just fallen asleep mid-conversation and was now snoring lightly. He mumbled something about the Pepper rule of needing naps now.

Beta looked around. "But why didn't you let us all know you were doing this, Mom?".

"I thought it would be a fun surprise." She smiled and waved her broom about. "Surprise! You know, I think I make a pretty great witch, if I do say so myself!"

Annie asked, "So we didn't curse the family when we broke the crystal ball?"

Meemaw guffawed. "The crystal ball was one of Presto's bestest worst tricks! He'd get a volunteer from the crowd and start telling their fortunes, then he'd smack that ball so it would roll off the table and shatter. Always made the crowd howl with laughter!"

Realization dawned on Beta. "Wait a minute. Presto made the ball shatter . . . on purpose?"

"Of course! Pappy was always in on the joke. He worked darn tootin' hard at being the worst magician—and best prop comedian—in the world! I'm surprised you didn't find the box of spare crystal balls. They're right behind the saw-a-person-in-half box." She winked at Annie. "Oh, and the stains on the saw-a-person-in-half

box are just prune juice. They always creeped me out, too."

Everyone laughed, most of all Beta. In the attic, he'd said he was more talented than Presto, but he'd had it wrong the whole time! Presto had been so talented that even now his magic was working. Beta could only hope to be as good an entertainer as his great-grandfather!

Beta raised his teacup to toast. "Well, here's to Presto, the Famously Terrible and the Terribly Famous Magician!"

Annie agreed happily, "I'll drink to that!"

The Peppers clinked teacups together and took a sip of Tee's herbal blend. They had to admit, Tee's tea was so fabulous, it was practically magical!

CHAPTER 11

Two days later, on Halloween night, the Peppers were dressed to party. They lined up in the front hallway of the house for a family picture before going out for some good old-fashioned trick-or-treating.

After the opening of Tee's Teas at the Black Cat Café, everyone had revised their costume ideas. Both Beta and Annie had dressed up like their newest hero, Presto Pepper. They each wore a top hat and satin cape from Presto's old wardrobe.

Tee hand-stitched a were-Chihuahua costume for Scoochy. Since she refused to stop acting like a dog anyway, Tee thought she might as well look the part. Of course, the family had made sure to give her a flea bath first.

Maria was dressed up in her space marine costume from *Vampire Lizard Mummymen from Mars*, and Megs was dressed as a vampire lizard mummyman (on crutches).

Sal had decided to stick with his zombie theme, since he mostly looked the part anyway. His mustache had even started growing in.

Tee wore the black witch dress and hat she'd worn at the opening of the café.

And naturally, Ricky was all decked out in the perfect vampire outfit, complete with cape, fangs, and pale white makeup. He'd invited Evelyn to trick-or-treat with them.

After the photo, they all waved goodbye to Meemaw, who wore an astronaut suit for the night. She had decided to stay behind and hand out candy to the trick-or-treaters.

Meemaw filled a basket with treats and set it by the door. Then she boiled a cup of Tee's tea and got comfortable at the dining room table.

"Would you believe that family of mine? They think curses are real and believe in vampires, zombies, and werewolves, no less!" She shook her head. "Kids these days have some strange ideas. That Beta in particular has got quite an imagination, but not a whole lot of detective sense. Never thought to ask how them shards from the ball kept making it down out of the attic, now, did he?"

The old woman slowly shuffled a deck of cards and set it on the table. "Let's play Go Fish. You cut, Pappy. But no tricks this time! I'm a-watching!"

The deck of cards floated into the air and separated into two clean piles.

Meemaw had to turn her hearing aid up to hear it, but she could just about make out a very quiet, very happy ghostly chuckle in the air.

The End?*

---

* No! The Peppers will be back in *The Pepper Party Double Dare Disguise*!

Can't get enough Pepper pandemonium? Read on for a sneak peak of this feisty family's next crazy catastrophe!

All the Peppers loaded into Sal's food truck, the Chili Chikka-Wow-Wow, to drive over to the convention.

All the Peppers except for one, that is.

The punishment for breaking Sal's prized

possession was harsh. There would be no Comic Con for Megs this year.

She had pleaded with her father. She had cried. Her mother and brothers and sisters had begged Sal to change his mind. They all knew how important meeting Centaura was to Megs.

Yet Sal wouldn't budge. "It's a Pepper rule: Trash a trophy, take a time-out!"

He didn't understand that this was a once-in-a-lifetime chance for Megs. Centaura had never come to San Pimento before. And she might never again. Megs might NEVER get to meet her!

But while *Megs Pepper* was forbidden from attending Comic Con, if she could come up with a clever enough disguise, her family would never know she was there!

MEET THE PEPPERS

FUNNY RUNS IN THE FAMILY.